Baby Bird

REW GIBBS • ZOSIENKA

For Tomene
With huge thanks
to B, J, R & L

In loving memory of Andrew.
Thank you for making this happen.

Brimming with creative inspiration, how-to projects, and useful information to enrich your everyday life, Quarto Knows is a favourite destination for those pursuing their interests and passions. Visit our site and dig deeper with our books into your area of interest: Quarto Creates, Quarto Cooks, Quarto Homes, Quarto Lives, Quarto Drives, Quarto Explores, Quarto Gifts, or Quarto Kids.

Text © 2018 The estate of Andrew Gibbs. Illustrations © 2018 Zosienka.
First Published in 2018 by Lincoln Children's Books,
an imprint of The Quarto Group.
The Old Brewery, 6 Blundell Street, London N7 9BH, United Kingdom.
T (0)20 7700 6700 F (0)20 7700 8066 www.QuartoKnows.com
This paperback edition published 2019
The right of Zosienka to be identified as the illustrator and Andrew Gibbs to be identified
as the author of this work has been asserted by them in accordance with the
Copyright, Designs and Patents Act, 1988 (United Kingdom).

A catalogue record for this book is available from the British Library.
ISBN 978-1-78603-592-9
The illustrations were created gouache paints.
Set in Baskerville
Published by Jenny Broom and Rachel Williams
Designed by Zoë Tucker
Edited by Katie Cotton and Kate Davies
Production by Jenny Cundill and Kate O'Riordan
Manufactured in Dongguan, China TL112018
9 8 7 6 5 4 3 2 1

MIX
Paper from
responsible sources
FSC® C104723
FSC
www.fsc.org

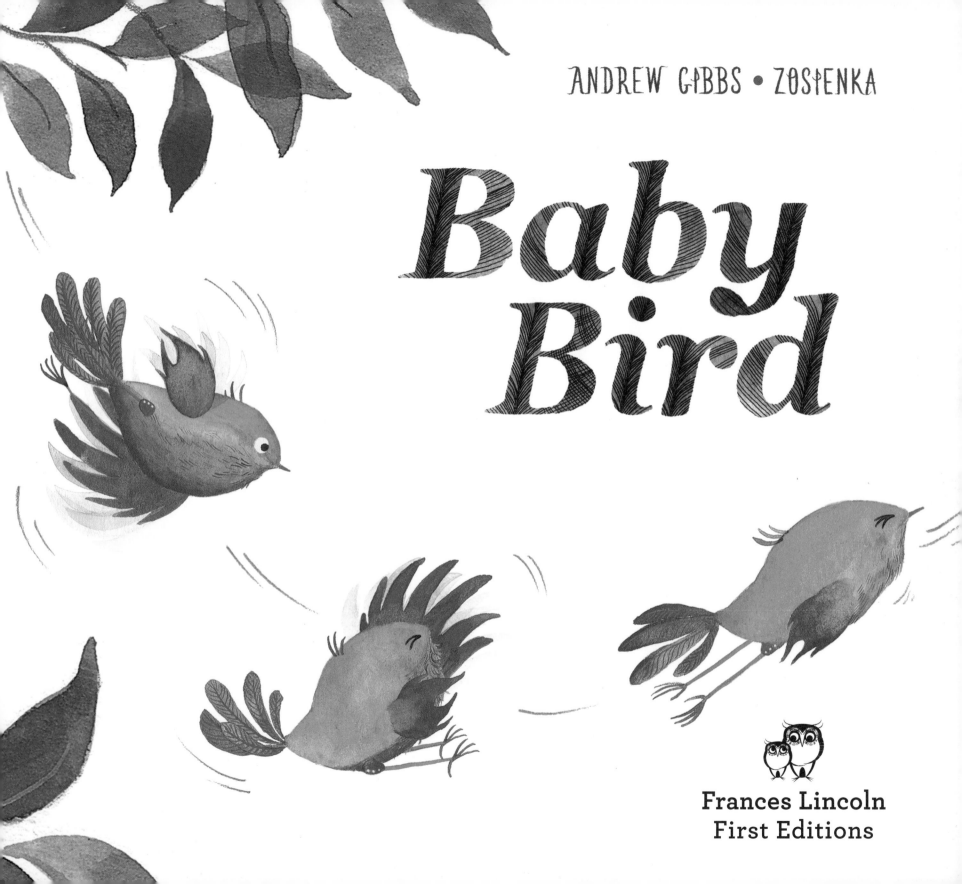

ANDREW GIBBS • ZOSIENKA

Baby Bird

Frances Lincoln
First Editions

Baby Bird was *different* from the other hatchlings. One of Baby's wings was twisted and shrunken and not at all like the other one.

Baby's brothers and sisters all had two matching
wings, and as time passed they grew bigger and stronger.

Soon the time came for the
hatchlings to leave the nest.
Baby watched the others
flap and fly away.

'Birds are born to fly,'
thought Baby. 'I suppose
it's now or never…'

So Baby took a big run up and yelled,
'Wait for me!'

Baby flapped…

grrr

—ahh!

and flapped...

and...

Baby watched the other hatchlings
swooping and laughing as
they played together.

'It's all so easy for them,' Baby thought.
But close by was a little bridge
and a soft patch of grass, and
it gave Baby an idea…

'That's the perfect spot to learn to fly!'

Baby practised flying
all morning.

Really, it was more like falling,
but Baby was determined.
'I'm not giving up!'

Suddenly Baby heard
a rustling in the bushes.
Something dark was moving
beneath the bridge...

In a flash, a shape burst from the
shadows and landed beak to beak with Baby.

'Aaaah!' Baby screamed. 'A monster!'

'Aaaah!
Where?
Where?!'

'Oh, *me*?' said the monster. 'I'm not a monster –
I'm Cooter! Nice to meet you! I've been
watching you jumping up and down over
and over again. Whaddya doing?'

'I'm not *jumping*,' said Baby.
'I'm *flying*. I just haven't quite got
the hang of it yet.'

Cooter spotted Baby's
little wing and gasped.
'Holy baloney!
What happened?'

'Nothing!' snapped Baby.
'Leave me alone!'

'Sorry,' said Cooter. 'I didn't mean
to make fun. But you might need a buddy
to help get you flying. Whaddya say?'

Baby thought about it for a while
and said, 'That would be great.'

Baby and Cooter practised flying all afternoon.

They tried the King Swing...

the Spring Launcher...

...and plain old jumping and flapping.
But nothing worked.

As the shadows grew long,
Baby decided to take a break.

'Never mind!' Cooter said. 'I sure am
having fun with you, anyway.
You wanna go swimming now?'

'I'm not *having fun!*' Baby exploded.

'And I don't want to swim! I'm not a fish. I'm a bird,
and I'm learning to fly, like all birds should,
so that I can join the others in the sky.'

Cooter looked sadly at Baby and said,
'I don't think you'll *ever* be able to fly with that little wing.'
Baby thought: 'Cooter's right. I am a baby bird.
I have a broken wing, and I'll *never* fly.'

Baby flopped down on the
bridge, feeling *very* tired…

and *very* sad
and *very* heavy…

But then…

Baby flapped…

and flapped…

'What am I going to do?'
cried Baby, safe on Cooter's back.
'I'm a bird. Birds are born to fly, but I can't.'

'Hey,' said Cooter. 'I'm a bird and I'm a *terrible* flier.'

'Really?' Baby gasped.

'Yep!' said Cooter.
'It's never bothered me.'

'I know what'll cheer you up,' said Cooter.
'Some good old-fashioned Coot Scooting. I've always
done it alone, but I sure think you'd love it.'

Baby frowned. 'What the heck is *Coot Scooting*?'
'I'll show ya!' said Cooter, spreading his wings.
'Hold on!'

Coot Scooting was frightening at first,
but soon, as the world whizzed by,
Baby forgot to be scared and started laughing.

'You know something?' said Cooter, laughing too.
'What?' yelled Baby, into the wind.

'You don't need
strong wings to fly.'

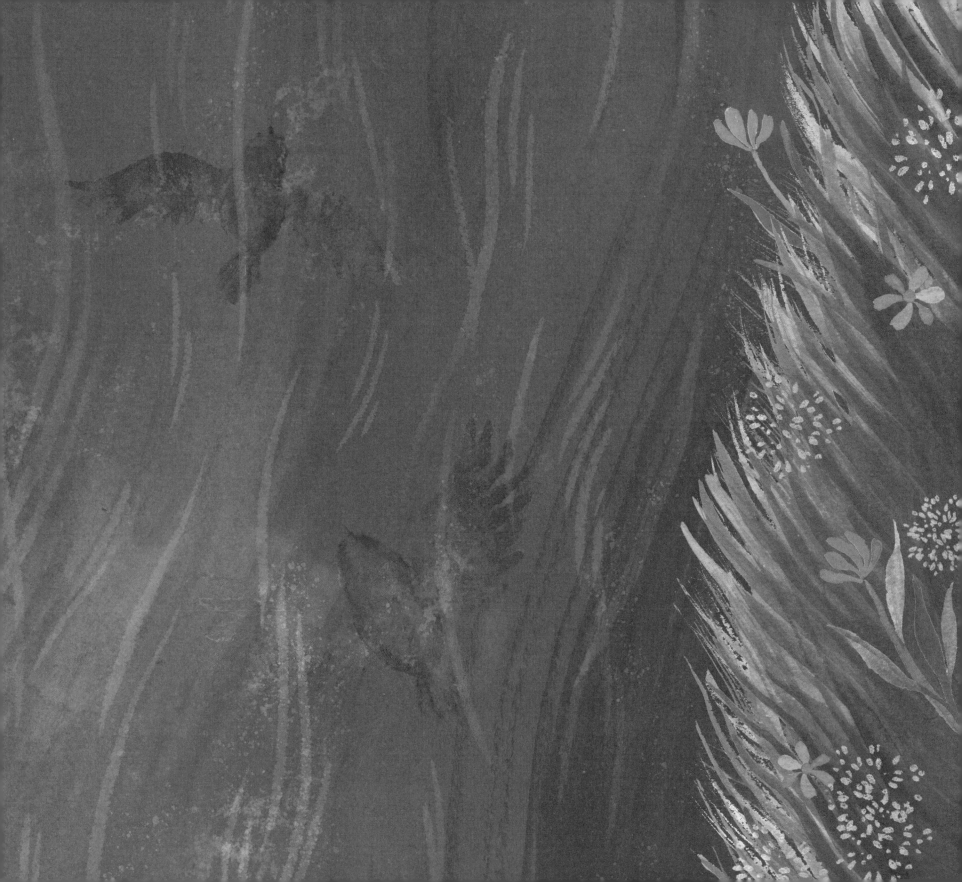

MALPAS

INTRODUCING FIRST EDITIONS, A NEW IMPRINT DEDICATED TO NEW PICTURE BOOK TALENT

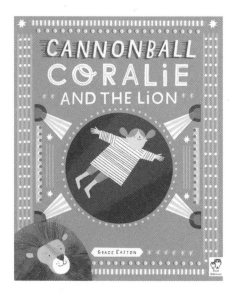

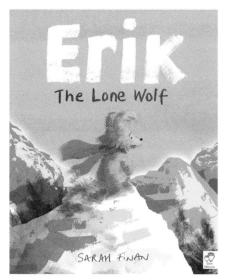

Cannonball Coralie and the Lion

ISBN: 978-1-78603-031-3

Coralie longs to join the circus – but the Man in the Big Hat says her tricks just aren't good enough. With the help of her new friend, Lion, Coralie realizes she's perfect just the way she is. A heartwarming picture book about friendship and the importance of standing up for yourself.

Erik the Lone Wolf

ISBN: 978-1-78603-010-8

Being a wolf means sticking with the pack. Everyone knows that – except for Erik, one little wolf cub who dreams of setting off on his own adventure…all by himself! But will life as a lone wolf be everything he hoped, or will he miss the rough and tumble of the pack?

The Best Sound in the World

ISBN: 978-1-78603-169-3

Roy is a lion. His favourite thing is catching sounds from all over the city, while trying to avoid his irritating neighbour, Jemmy. One day Roy sets off to find the best sound in the world. He travels far and wide, becoming more and more confused, but when he learns that Jemmy has come with him, will he realise that perhaps friendship is the best thing of all?

If All the World Were…

ISBN: 978-1-78603-059-7

A moving, lyrical picture book about a young girl's love for her granddad and how she copes when he dies, written by poet and playwright Joseph Coelho. This powerful and ultimately uplifting text is the ideal way to introduce children to the concept of death and dying, particularly children who have lost a grandparent.

Frances Lincoln
First Editions